An Itty Bitty
Christmas

PAGE PUBLISHING, INC.
New York, NY

First originally published by Page Publishing, Inc. 2018

ISBN 978-1-64138-839-9 (Hardcover)
ISBN 978-1-64138-840-5 (Digital)

Printed in the United States of America

An Itty Bitty Christmas

Karen Nowicki

Itty Bitty is a young, happy, brown-and-white Jack Russell Terrier, who lives on a small farm in Maine. She has her human mom and dad and her big brother, Chris, to care for her. Living with them are two horses, Czaro and Tenor, as well as flock of chickens. Itty Bitty loves Mom and Dad's twin daughters, Kate and Steph. Steph's German shepherd, Sabre, is a playmate of Itty Bitty and Chris. They do not live on the farm, so Itty Bitty doesn't get to see them very often. It is always special when they are together.

One December morning, Mom called to Itty Bitty and Chris. "We are going to get our Christmas tree today."

Itty Bitty looked at Chris and asked, "What's a Christmas tree?"

Chris looked at her and said, with all the knowledge of an older brother, "It's a tree they put in the house and add lights and decorations to."

Itty Bitty cocked her head to one side. "Why?"

"I don't know," Chris said. "Come on, let's get into the truck. I'll race you!"

As Itty Bitty and Chris climbed into the front seat of the truck and into Mom's lap, Itty Bitty thought about Christmas trees. *They must be wonderful things*, she thought. Mom and Dad were singing and laughing and holding hands.

When they arrived at the tree farm, Itty Bitty looked at all the trees and wondered how they were going to pick a Christmas tree. There were so many! Rows and rows of trees! Each one tall, green, and perfect. They were all beautiful!

Itty Bitty wandered but kept an eye on Dad and Mom as they walked around. She didn't understand why they wanted a tree. There were a lot of trees in the woods around the farm. Why were these trees special? Yes, they were all very pretty, but the trees at home were pretty too, even now with leaves all gone.

Finally, Dad said, "This one."

Mom nodded in agreement, smiling.

Dad took his saw, and in a few minutes, the Christmas tree was in the back of the truck, and the little family was on their way.

Once they arrived back home, Itty Bitty was astonished when Dad *really* brought the tree into the house. She had thought Chris was teasing her! Mom brought down boxes from the attic, and they began to decorate the tree. This was fun to Itty Bitty, and when the tree was all done, it danced with blinky lights, colorful balls, and ornaments.

As Christmas Day grew closer, Itty Bitty was still confused about all the excitement. Mom and Dad were whistling and singing, making up silly songs and seemed happier than usual. They were full of hugs and kisses for Chris and Itty Bitty. A pile of shopping bags grew in the not-so-secret hiding place in the bedroom. It snowed outside. Then, Aunts Kate and Steph, along with Sabre, came to the farm with packages and secrets of their own.

Chris and Sabre romped around the yard, but Itty Bitty just watched. Her curiosity grew. "What is all this?" she asked herself. "I wish I knew what was so special." She pawed at Mom, who picked her up to snuggle and gave her a kiss.

"Christmas is a special time," Mom told Itty Bitty. "It's about the Christ child being born, family, giving presents, and togetherness. Mostly, though, it's about love."

Itty Bitty sat on the back of her chair and pondered this.

Who is the Christ child? Presents? For whom? Togetherness and love. I know about those. She looked out at Chris and Sabre as they played in the snow. *I think I will go out and togetherness now,* Itty Bitty said to herself.

And she ran out to join them.

That night was Christmas Eve. The entire family was together — Mom, Dad, Steph, Kate, Chris, Sabre, and Itty Bitty. They turned off all the house lights, leaving only the Christmas tree blinking happily to light up the room. Music played softly, and each of the people talked about their favorite Christmases. Except Mom. She said that this one was her favorite because they were all together. Itty Bitty looked and saw tears shining in Mom's eyes. She climbed up and gently licked them away. She didn't know they were happy tears.

This made Itty Bitty think more about Christmas. Once again, she was curious. *Why was this so special?*

As the hour grew late, Dad said it was time to go to bed. After all, what if Santa Claus came and everyone was still awake? Kate and Steph laughed happily as they scrambled up and raced to their rooms. Sabre, barking like a silly puppy, ran with them. Chris and Itty Bitty hopped into bed with Mom and Dad. Chris snuggled under the covers, but Itty Bitty laid down on top.

Did Dad say Santa Claus? she thought. *What is a Santa Claus? And the Christ child? Who is that? What do they have to do with Christmas?* She rested her head on her paws. I wish I understood. She sighed and closed her eyes.

Then, something woke her up! "*Woof*!" Itty Bitty said.

Dad put a gentle hand on her. "It's okay, girl," he said in his sleep.

But Itty Bitty was wide awake now. She decided she would get up and make sure everything was okay. She hopped off the bed and went out into the living room. There was someone there! Someone was next to the tree. Itty Bitty tried to bark to wake up Dad and Mom, but she was so scared that she couldn't! Then the intruder turned around.

"Don't be frightened, Itty Bitty," he said. "There is nothing to be afraid of. I'm Santa Claus. Didn't your Dad say I was coming tonight?"

Itty Bitty looked at Santa and nodded, finally finding her voice. "Yes, Dad said you were coming." She looked at Santa's red suit and white beard, his rosy cheeks and kind eyes. He was smiling at her. Santa sat down and held out a hand to her.

Cautiously, Itty Bitty stepped up to Santa and thought he smelled like cookies.

"I understand you are having trouble understanding Christmas," he said.

"Yes," Itty Bitty answered. "Mom and Dad are very happy, especially with Kate and Steph here. Then there's this tree, all these packages, and you!" Itty Bitty took a breath. "And Mom said something about a child being born. I am very confused."

Santa smiled, nodded, and picked her up. "Yes, I can see where you might not understand all this, but let me try to help you."

"First of all, it is okay if you don't understand all of this. You don't have to. All you need to do is believe. Christmas means many different things to every person. You know that I am Santa Claus. I travel the entire world on Christmas Eve, giving special gifts to all the good boys and girls."

"And puppies too?"

"And puppies too," Santa chuckled. "I know your mom is happy because she has her whole family together. That is what makes her happiest of all. Your dad is happy for the same reason and because your mom is so happy. Christmas can be a time when even grown-ups can be a little bit like a child. Or at least feel like one.

"The Christmas tree, in your family, is here to show hope for new life. In the winter, the outside can be very white and grey and brown, but trees like this are always green. It is a reminder of spring in the winter. The decorations on your tree are all about the family. Most of them are from when they were all children. Even your Mom and Dad.

"But, Itty Bitty, as your mom said, Christmas is mostly about the birth of a very special child. This child is the son of God. He will grow up to be an amazing man whose love will heal the world of sin. Christmas is the celebration of His birth. People give gifts to honor Him and to symbolize the gifts that three kings brought to this baby."

"Was this baby a prince? He must have been since he was visited by kings."

"No, Itty Bitty. He wasn't a prince. In fact, he was born in a stable. There was no palace."

Itty Bitty was now even more confused. She thought about this baby who would be an "amazing man," this baby who was born in a stable, the son of God. "How can all this be?" she asked.

Santa thought a moment. "Magic, miracles, and love, Itty Bitty. There is no way to explain it except those three words. Sometimes you just need to believe." Santa looked at Itty Bitty and saw she was still struggling to understand. He smiled. "I can show you, if you wish. I have a very special gift to deliver there."

"Will we be back by morning?" she asked. "I don't want to miss Christmas."

"Yes, we will be. I promise."

Itty Bitty nodded.

Santa held her close to his red coat. "Don't be afraid. I will take care of you. Close your eyes and believe."

Itty Bitty looked up at Santa. "Believe? Believe in what?"

Santa chuckled. "You are a funny little pup. For now, just believe in me."

Itty Bitty smiled back at him. "That's easy." She closed her eyes and snuggled into Santa's cozy arms.

She heard a whoosh, like horses breathing, felt a warm breeze on her nose and then all was still and silent.

"It's okay, Itty Bitty," Santa said. "Open your eyes."

Itty Bitty opened her eyes and saw she was in a barn. There were cows, sheep, and a tired little donkey resting in a warm stall. The hay and straw smelled sweet and fresh. Itty Bitty jumped down from Santa's arms and cautiously wandered over toward a manger, where a man and woman knelt. Itty Bitty stopped a few feet away, uncertain if she should get any nearer. She heard a tiny coo come from the golden hay and desperately wanted to see inside. She took another step, her paw quietly rustling the straw on the floor. The man and woman turned to look at Itty Bitty. She looked back at them and took a timid step closer. The woman reached to Itty Bitty and offered to pet her. Itty Bitty stepped quickly into the outstretched hand, her fear gone. Mary's touch was soft and gentle and warm. As Itty Bitty leaned into the palm, she was suddenly reminded of her own mom and felt an overwhelming love.

"Would you like to see the baby?" Santa asked. Itty Bitty, unable to speak, nodded. She stepped over to the manger, but it was too tall for her, so Santa picked her up and held her to the side of the wooden feed box.

There, in the soft hay, was a tiny baby. His face peaked out from a woolen blanket. His eyes were open and looking at Itty Bitty. She looked back at him and believed. There *was* a magic about this baby that Itty Bitty couldn't understand, but all of a sudden, it didn't matter. She didn't have to understand. She could just believe. Still, not able to utter a word, Itty Bitty looked back at Santa, wonder in her eyes.

He smiled at her. "Now you see why it is so hard to describe the Christmas miracle?"

Itty Bitty nodded and, looking back at the baby, smiled.

"Itty Bitty, it is time for us to go home," Santa said. He stood up with Itty Bitty in his arms. She looked back at the Christ child and saw the golden glow of a halo around His head. He was still looking at her. She felt His love and Santa's warm touch. She sighed happily and closed her eyes.

Then, she was back home. Santa was gently placing her on the bed next to Mom.

"Santa," Itty Bitty asked, sleepily, "what was the special gift you had to deliver?"

Santa softly touched her face. "Sweet Itty Bitty, YOU were the gift I had to deliver," he whispered. He kissed her head, and then Santa disappeared.

Christmas day arrived bright and snowy. Itty Bitty was surprised at how many presents were under the tree. Everybody, even Chris, Sabre, and herself, received gifts. Itty Bitty had one very special present under the tree—a red heart-shaped tag for her collar with just one word on it...

An Itty Bitty Press Publication

About the Author

Karen Nowicki lives in Lyman, Maine, a quintessential small town. She lives on a little horse farm where she and her husband, Bill, tend to the horses, chickens, their careers, and of course Itty Bitty and her older brother Chris. Karen is an avid dressage rider, photographer, and outdoorswoman. She can usually be found out in the barn, out on the riding trails, taking photos of anything and everything, or sitting down smothered in Jack Russell terriers. Karen and Bill have twin daughters, Kate and Steph who both live and work in Maine. Steph has a German shepherd, Sabre (who is much bigger than Itty Bitty), and he will appear in other adventures. Karen's passion for photography and all things outdoors, as well as having two Jack Russell's as constant companions, led to the inevitable— "this would make a great book, Eureka!" moment. Karen's first Book, *Itty Bitty After the Rain*, is a Book Excellence Award finalist.

CPSIA information can be obtained
at www.ICGtesting.com
Printed in the USA
BVHW02*1444170418
513564BV00001B/1/P

9 781641 388399